Little Bear's New Friend

A Little Animal Adventure

Little Bear's New Friend

Written by Muriel Pépin
Adapted by Deborah Kovacs
Illustrations by Marcelle Geneste

Published by The Reader's Digest Association Limited
London ❖ New York ❖ Sydney ❖ Montreal

It was late autumn and a family of brown bears had gone back home to their cave for a long winter nap. But the littlest bear wasn't feeling a bit sleepy.

'I don't want to stay inside,' he told his mum. 'This is such a little cave. I'll get so bored staying inside all winter!'

'Dear little bear,' said Mother Bear. 'You won't be bored. You'll be asleep. Bears spend the winter sleeping.'

So the little bear cub curled up with his family in the snug cave. But when the others began to snore, the little bear cub's eyes were still wide open. He tip-toed to the entrance and stared out in wonderment as the first snow of winter covered the ground in a thick white blanket.

'Snow! Real snow!' he cried in delight, watching the fluffy flakes fall all around him. He had heard about snow but had never before seen it. He had to investigate. Quietly he crept outside.

'Br-r-r! This snow is COLD!' said the little bear cub, patting it with his furry paws. 'And it's so WHITE!' He had to blink to get his eyes used to the brightness.

'And it's so BEAUTIFUL!' The little bear ran through the trees at full speed delighted with the swirling flakes all around him. Then he began to roll, over and over again in the soft new snow.

Before long, the little bear cub had run and jumped and twirled and spun around so much that he didn't know where his cave was anymore. 'Mummy,' he cried. 'I'm lost!'

Then he heard a voice he didn't recognise.
He looked up and saw a furry little wolf cub
who was no bigger than him and looked very
friendly.

'Are you lost?' asked the wolf cub. 'I know
these woods. I can show you the way home but
will you play with me first?'

The little bear was so pleased to find a friend and time flew as they played happily together. The wolf cub showed the bear how to make snowballs and how to slide across the frozen pond. Then they both lay down and got up again – delighting in the wolf and bear-shaped imprints their furry bodies left in the snow.

The little bear was having such a
good time that he completely forgot
about finding his cave and going back
to his mother.

But Mother Bear had not forgotten about her little cub. She woke up and when she saw he was missing, she bounded outside. 'Where is my little bear?' she cried. 'These woods are full of danger. He could be injured or even eaten by a big, bad wolf!'

Just then, who should appear but a fierce she-wolf! The two mothers stared at each other, bared their teeth and growled. Then they heard gun shots - BANG, BANG, BANG!

'Hunters!' they cried and ran for cover behind the same rock.

When the hunters had gone past, Mother Bear turned to the wolf, quite forgetting that they were usually enemies.

'I'm looking for my little bear,' she said. 'He sneaked out this morning to play and I haven't seen him since!'

'So did my little cub,' said Mother Wolf. 'I'm so worried about him!'

At once the two mothers set out to search the snowy woods. Together they covered the ground much more quickly than if they had worked alone.

'Look!' said Mother Wolf. 'My little cub's paw prints!'

'And, look!' said Mother Bear. 'There are my cub's paw prints, too! Let's follow them. They must have been playing together.'

Over rocks and stones, up and down hills, the two mothers followed their cubs' snowy tracks until they suddenly arrived, their hearts pounding … back at the entrance of the bears' family cave!

Inside was an astonishing sight! The little grey wolf cub was sound asleep, snuggled up in the midst of a pile of snoring bear cubs.

'It looks as if my little bear has found a new friend,' said Mother Bear happily.
'And my little wolf has found the cosiest place in the forest for a winter nap!' replied Mother Wolf.

All about ... BEARS

LITTLE AND LARGE!

When a brown bear cub is born, it is small enough to fit in your hand. Cubs live with their mother for two years and she teaches them everything they need to know to survive on their own. Bear cubs grow quickly – an adult can be as much as 2.5 metres tall!

SNOW BEARS

Not all bears are brown. Polar bears, who live in the Arctic where summers are short and winters are long, have white coats that make them difficult to see against the snow.

FACT FILE

SWEET TREATS

Almost all bears love honey. They take apart beehives full of honey with their big paws and don't seem to mind the angry bees swarming around them. Their thick skin and fur protect them from stings.

Did you know?

BEARS IN ACTION
Bears are very powerful animals. They will move heavy rocks and even split old tree trunks in order to find the insects they feed on.

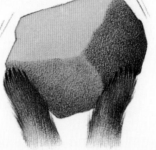

SHAKE, SHAKE, SHAKE!
Bears are also very good at climbing trees. Once up they'll shake a branch so that nuts or fruits fall to the ground, then they scramble down for a feast.

A LONG WINTER SLEEP
Many bears sleep for most of the winter. A mother bear will find a cosy cave and settle down with her cubs for a long sleep until the warm weather comes.

Little Bear's New Friend is a Little Animal Adventures book
published by Reader's Digest Young Families, Inc.
by arrangement with Éditions Nathan, Paris, France

Written by Muriel Pépin
Adapted by Deborah Kovacs
Illustrations by Marcelle Geneste
Notebook artwork © Paul Bommer

This edition was adapted and published in 2008 by
The Reader's Digest Association Limited
11 Westferry Circus, Canary Wharf, London E14 4HE

® Reader's Digest, the Pegasus logo and Reader's Digest Young Families
are registered trademarks of
The Reader's Digest Association, Inc.

We are committed to both the quality of our products
and the service we provide to our customers.
We value your comments, so please feel free to contact us on
08705 113366 or via our website at:
www.readersdigest.co.uk
If you have any comments or suggestions about the content of our books,
you can contact us at: gbeditorial@readersdigest.co.uk

Printed in China.

Book code: 637-002 UP0000-2
ISBN: 978 0 276 44232 2